WAKE UP,

CITY!

by Alvin Tresselt
Pictures by Roger Duvoisin

Lothrop, Lee & Shepard Co., New York

Under the stars the city sleeps.
Only a policeman is about, walking past the street lamp.
Only an alley cat, prowling a backyard fence.
Only a mother, singing her baby back to sleep.

Then slowly the eastern sky begins to brighten.
Here a light goes on . . . there a light goes on . . .
The city sparrows begin to cheep.
And the ducks on the pond in the park call to each other
across the black water.

The city is waking in the dim gray dawn-light.

The policeman sniffs the fresh morning air.

"Ahh, a fine day it will be today," he says to himself.

The night train from far away pulls into the station,
full of sleepy people.

In the garage the buses are ready for their day's work.
Their gas tanks are full and their windshields are clean.
The bus drivers straighten their caps and hop into the buses.

In the harbor a great ocean liner
comes in on the morning tide.
Busy tugboats pull it up to the pier.

Down in the noisy markets men are loading trucks with food.
Crates of lettuce and carrots.
Boxes of oranges, bags of onions.
Fruits and vegetables from the farms.
Fresh food for the city to eat.

As the policeman walks back to his station house
he hears the *brrring* of alarm clocks.
A radio voice tells him today will be fair and cooler.
And he hears the babies crying for their breakfast.

With a clank and a crunch and a rumble
the garbage trucks grind through the streets.
A sprinkler truck leaves a trail of shiny wet pavemen
to catch the pink sky overhead.

The corner store is open, with stacks of crisp newspapers
piled up in front.
Fair and cooler, says the weather report, with moderate winds.
Barometer steady.

SODA-LUNCHEONETTE

CIGARS CIGARETTES

Coca Cola

CANDY

9ve

Ice Cream

Soda 10c

From open windows comes the smell of perking coffee
and sizzling bacon.
The pop of toasters, and the voices of mothers calling
"Hurry up, you'll be late!"

Now the streets hum with the hustle and bustle and jostle
of the traffic.
With a honk and a toot and a start and a stop
the trucks and buses and taxis crowd through the busy streets.

Fathers are hurrying to their offices.
Mothers are making beds and washing dishes.
And the children have left for school.
Another day has begun.

GOOD MORNING!